THE NANNY'S CHRISTMAS WISH

SNOWBOUND IN SAWYER CREEK

LACY WILLIAMS

lacy williams

CHAPTER 1

"HOLY MISTLETOE."

Amber Moore gulped as she took in the glittering white lights on the floor-to-twenty-foot-ceiling fir.

She'd known her friend Mallory Trudeau was rich. Mallory and her brother Cash owned the Double Cross ranch in Caldwell county, not far from Austin, Texas.

But this was... ostentatious.

Not usually a word that Amber associated with her friend. Mallory was down-to-earth and as nice as they came. When Amber had shown up in Sawyer Creek eighteen months ago with only a backpack to her name, Mallory had taken her under her wing and helped her find a nanny job

LACY WILLIAMS

for a nearby rancher, a live-in one. And Mallory had given her a character reference when Amber couldn't provide any references of her own.

Amber owed Mallory a lot. And Mallory never seemed to want to collect. Which worked for Amber, who had no way to pay her back anyway. Except it worried her.

When would her bill come due?

Nothing came for free.

She let her gaze drift to the large picture windows, where snowflakes swirled and battered against the glass. Surely the storm would let up soon. They were only supposed to have gotten a dusting of snow this evening. Not a storm.

Amber pulled her gaze away from the window and the snowstorm, which was only stressing her out, and focused on Mallory. "How many years has your family hosted the Christmas ball?"

She let her gaze sweep the room, looking for her boss, Jace. She was an expert at multi-tasking. Nannies—and moms—had to be.

"My grandma threw the first Cattlemen's Association Christmas Ball forty years ago," Mallory said. "We've held it here almost every year."

Because Mallory's family had a legacy.

Amber had no legacy, and she'd rather forget the history she did have.

She blinked away those thoughts. Holidays always made her morose, thinking about what she'd never had.

And they made her angry.

Anger had no place at a party like this.

Neither did Amber.

She was pretty sure that everyone in the room could tell she was a fraud. Even the twinkling crystals strung through evergreen boughs seemed to mock her.

She'd spent her entire Christmas bonus—the one she'd never expected, the one that had made her cry—on this dress. She'd driven all the way to Austin to a high-end salon to have her hair styled in this intricate updo she'd never be able to replicate in a million years. She'd even had her makeup and nails done, a treat she'd never dared spoil herself with.

She'd really wanted to look like she belonged.

Because then maybe Jace would notice her.

But she kept getting looks from the other women, and some of the younger men, that made her think she'd gotten it wrong. Again.

LACY WILLIAMS

"Ladies."

Amber jumped.

She'd recognize Jace's voice in a pitch-black cave filled with rushing water.

She wasn't ready.

But there he was, towering over her and looking more handsome than she'd ever imagined in a tuxedo jacket—no tie—and boots. His shoulders went on for miles. Broad enough for Bo to snuggle into when he jumped into his father's arms.

Her face flamed.

This was her chance to show Jace that she wasn't just a nanny, she was a woman.

His brown eyes barely flicked over her.

Say something witty, Amber. Say something. Anything.

She couldn't catch her breath.

He pushed a glass of champagne in her direction and handed one to Mallory, too, which meant he hadn't been thinking specifically of Amber.

"You look nice tonight." His words seemed to encompass them both.

Amber's heart sank even as her exposed chest and throat burned hotter. She didn't drink. Jace didn't know that, and she didn't want him to feel awkward, but she didn't know what to do with the flute. She held it away from her body and wrapped her other arm around her middle, cupping her elbow.

This was a disaster. She'd spent upwards of five hundred bucks to get ready for tonight, and he wasn't even looking at her.

Say something.

He was staring across the room, and she grasped for something, anything to catch his attention.

"Thanks for giving me the night off." How lame could she be? But now her mouth wouldn't stop moving. "Did Bo have any trouble with the sitter?"

Jace's face softened the way she'd come to recognize over the year-plus she'd worked for him. He loved his son deeply—a feeling she identified with. Bo was special.

Now Jace stopped scanning the room and looked directly at Amber for the first time. "Other than complaining for the seven hundredth time that you are 'way more fun' than Mrs. Ritter, he was fine."

Her heart pinched in a good way. The same

way it did every time Bo did something to show that he cared about her. "Good."

And then she became tongue-tied again.

"The music just started," Mallory said. Amber had forgotten her friend was even standing there. "You two should catch a dance."

Amber's face flamed hotter. She glanced at the parquet dance floor, a mix of uncertainty and excitement thrilling through her. She had no idea how to dance. And hardly anyone was out there. Only two elderly couples.

But she'd dance with Jace anyway.

He blinked. As if the idea of dancing hadn't even occurred to him. "I don't think so."

He raised his champagne glass to salute them and excused himself.

Oh gosh. Double gosh.

Tears pricked her eyes, and Amber had to turn away so the same people who kept looking at her wouldn't see. She knew the tip of her nose was turning red—it always did when she cried.

She widened her eyes. Blinked, trying to stem the flow.

Mallory didn't say anything, even though she could've. She was such a good friend. Better than Amber deserved.

Maybe it was time. "I have to give up, don't I?"

Mallory winced. "He's either really oblivious, or..."

Or he doesn't want you.

Amber blinked harder. Her hope was spiraling hard. "I've been waiting for him to notice my existence, but if he can't see me in *this dress*...?" She was more of a jeans and T-shirt kind of girl. Amber shook her head. "Maybe he's just too polite to tell me I'm not his type."

She waited for Mallory's agreement. Amber *wasn't* Jace's type. He didn't know her at all, thought she was something completely different...

Even though she'd tried so hard to be a woman he'd want.

Mallory was distracted. Amber followed her gaze to a striking cowboy across the room who'd put her friend on high alert.

Amber didn't need to bother her friend with her problems. Not on a magical night like this one.

"I think I might go home," Amber said quietly. "Before the weather gets any worse."

Mallory's gaze snapped back to her. "Oh, you can't!"

Amber's tears were still too close to the surface. Her eyes felt hot, the skin stretched too tightly across her face.

Mallory's hand closed over hers. "Don't give up yet. At least stay for the party. Give him a chance to see the dress in all its glory. Dance with some other guys. Make him jealous."

Jace would have to be interested to be jealous, wouldn't he?

And which of these other guys would want to dance with *her*?

But Mallory was watching her with an intense look, and Amber knew her friend wasn't going to just drop it.

She could sneak out when Mallory got distracted again.

"Okay. I'll stay. For a while."

Jace Cantrell walked away from Amber, glad he hadn't worn a tie.

He already felt like he was suffocating.

He waded through the ocean of friends and acquaintances, nodding and smiling even though he'd rather be at home, reading fifty-seven books to Bo before bedtime.

How long until he could get out of here? At least the snowstorm brewing outside would make it an early evening. Up until a few seconds ago, his mind had been on the chores still waiting for him when he got home—including checking on the Golden Retriever puppies his neighbor had talked him into caring for while the Nelson family traveled for the holiday.

Everyone had the Christmas spirit, except him. He'd been pretending since Patricia's death two years ago. In the beginning, it'd been all he could do to just *breathe*. Christmas and all the trappings had been last on his list.

Something inside him had come back to life tonight. With a vengeance.

And it was because of Amber.

Which was a disaster.

She was his son's nanny. His employee.

Not to mention about a decade his junior.

It wasn't fair that the first spike of attraction he'd felt since Patricia's death was directed at a woman one who was off-limits.

What was she doing wearing a dress like that? The red sheath hugged her slim curves and highlighted just how fair her skin was.

He swallowed hard, bellying up to the bar

where both champagne and coffee were being served.

"Could I have a glass of ice water?" he asked the bartender.

He didn't need to dull his senses. He needed to cool off.

That *dress*. He'd barely been able to keep his eyes off of her.

Lecher.

Why did it have to be *her*?

He couldn't afford to mess up a good thing. She'd come along when he'd needed someone desperately. She'd become indispensable in his son's life.

Bo would be lost without her.

Which meant that Jace couldn't screw things up. The fact that he'd discovered just how attractive she was didn't matter. Couldn't.

She was nothing like Patricia.

He tried to dredge up the grief that had been so overwhelming in the beginning.

But after two years, what he felt was... sadness. He doubted the ache would ever go away completely.

But it no longer felt like he was drowning.

Had he moved on without even meaning to?

He'd quickly found in those first dark days that he couldn't afford to stay in bed. Bo had to eat. Three meals a day. And his son never missed it when Jace didn't eat, too, so he forced himself to join his son at meals and swallow a few bites even when he'd had no hunger pangs.

And the ranch didn't run itself. Animals needed to be fed. They couldn't care for themselves, and Patricia would've kicked his butt—even from the grave—if he'd squandered the savings they'd worked so hard to put away for Bo's future.

So he'd worked, even though he'd had to numbly fight his way through it.

Then Bo's maternal grandmother had offered to bring Bo to live with her because Jace had to work such long hours on the ranch.

He'd hired Amber within the week. She'd been a godsend when he'd needed her most.

And he would not repay her by hitting on her. She needed to feel safe in her workplace, which happened to be his home. And hers.

He gulped his water.

It didn't help.

He turned to face the room.

Chuck Randolf approached the bar.

Jace nodded his hello. He was four or five years the man's senior. Chuck owned a small spread on the other side of town.

Jace didn't know the man well, which is why he was surprised when Chuck sidled up, a glass in hand.

"Cantrell. Happy holidays."

"Same to you," Jace answered.

"How'd your alfalfa crop fare this year?"

Jace forced a smile. Chuck was a distraction. He could use one of those right now.

"A little dry this summer, but we made it all right. The herd should be fine for the winter."

Jace hadn't grown up on a ranch. His mom and dad had lived in the city—still did—but he'd read so many westerns as a kid that he'd begged his parents to send him to a summer camp hosted on a working ranch. He'd fallen in love with the life.

"And you?" He had to keep his mind from wandering, because it kept wanting to wander right back in Amber's direction...

"It might be a little tight this winter," Chuck said. "I've made it through worse."

Ranching was certainly a fickle business. One year you might break even. The next, go in the hole. And if you were really lucky, you might have a banner year.

But Jace had never wanted to do anything else.

"I was wondering..." Chuck scratched the back of his neck and, if Jace wasn't mistaken, flushed a little.

He waited for whatever was coming. The community of Sawyer Creek helped each other. Chuck was probably going to ask to use his tractor or some such—although the man did live kind of far away for a borrow like that.

"Do you know if Miss Moore is seeing anybody?"

"Amber?" Jace asked dumbly. Of course the man meant Amber. Jace had noticed her tonight. Why wouldn't other guys?

And Jace realized he didn't know. *Was* there someone she cared about?

"I don't know," Jace said. "But I take it you're interested?"

The other man shifted his boots. "Yeah, I... I am. She taught my niece in Sunday school a while back, and..." Chuck scratched that itch again.

No. Jace squelched the jealous voice that wanted to shut the man down.

He took a good look at him. Chuck was all right. Somebody Jace had known casually for years. The age gap between him and Amber wasn't too big.

The only thing making Jace want to squash him like a bug was his own jealousy.

Which was out-of-place, considering he hadn't even noticed Amber as a woman before tonight.

"So what do you want? My blessing?" he grated out.

Chuck's skin had gone from a healthy tan to cherry-red. "No, I—" He sounded almost strangled.

It was almost enough for Jace to feel sorry for him. Almost.

Chuck took a deep breath. Braced himself. "I've had this problem since, well... forever."

What?

"I can't talk to women. Especially pretty ones. I get all jammed up, and it's really awkward."

"So, you want an introduction?" This was getting better and better. *No way.*

"I was hoping you'd... I don't know. Woo her a little for me and then introduce me."

Like Cyrano de Bergerac?

Instinctively, Jace reached up and touched his nose.

Nope. Normal-sized honker.

It might've been a good fifteen years since high school, but he remembered the play they'd been forced to read in English class. Mostly because Patricia had loved the romance.

He'd just thought Cyrano was a loser.

And now Chuck was asking for his help.

Chuck watched him with a look that was both hopeful and knowing. Like he expected Jace to reject his request outright.

"You've got to be kidding, man," Jace said.

He did feel a little sorry for the guy, but...

He let his gaze wander over the crowd, because his crazy awareness of Amber hadn't gone away, and he knew right where she was standing, half-out of sight behind the huge Christmas tree.

She was talking with an older woman. Mrs. Pickles—no, Mrs. Pritchard. She was a librarian, one who read to the kids in a reading hour every week. The kids called her Mrs. Pickles.

Amber was smiling at something the older woman had said, the

lights from the tree catching golden high-lights in her hair.

She deserved someone special in her life, didn't she? A love like the one he'd shared with Patricia.

And it couldn't be him. He knew that better than anyone else.

Why shouldn't it be Chuck?

But really. Why did he have to be the "helper" here?

Maybe it was a good thing. If he set her up with Chuck, his attraction for her would have to wane, wouldn't it?

He rubbed one hand down his face, suddenly weary.

"Look, I don't know if she's seeing someone. I can ask. Maybe tell her some things about you. But I'm not going to romance her for you, all right?"

Chuck lit up.

And Jace felt a little like he'd been punched in the gut.

"Once I get going, you come over and introduce yourself, got it?"

Chuck nodded enthusiastically.

Jace set his shoulders and started to find a way through the crowd.

What had he just signed up for?

CHAPTER 2

WHAT THE HOLLY WAS HE DOING?

Jace's palms had gone sweaty and his heart was racing as he made his way through the crowded ballroom toward Amber.

Chuck must've hypnotized him or something, because he'd never done anything like this before.

He'd never had any game. Not even back in high school.

Patricia had been the one who'd done the asking out. After their first date—to a local diner —she'd told him when to call her.

And he'd followed through. Which led to her telling him to pick her up the next Friday evening for the high school basketball game.

He had.

And the rest was history.

After that initial period of awkwardness, everything with Patricia had been easy.

He'd never felt this sweaty before.

And he hadn't even reached Amber.

Oh, crap. There she was.

Mrs. Pickles had just walked away, and Amber turned a slow circle... and spotted him.

There was no changing his mind. No hiding. If he turned and walked away now, it'd be rude.

"Hey," he greeted her.

"Hey." She smiled, and he couldn't help noticing the slight indent in the left side of her cheek. Not quite a dimple, but a perfect place to leave a kiss.

What was he thinking?

Chuck.

He had to focus on Chuck.

But he also couldn't just lay it out there. He needed to warm her up, first.

"I saw you over here looking a little lonely," he said.

Her smile faltered. "Oh, I—" Something passed behind her eyes, an emotion he couldn't place.

Why had he said that?

"Actually, I saw you over here with Mrs. Pickles, and I was coming to the rescue. Once she starts talking, she doesn't stop."

Amber's gaze flitted away, her lashes descending to hide her eyes. Something about her smile was... off. "Oh, I don't mind Mrs. P. She recommended a couple of books that Bo might like. When I was little—" She abruptly cut herself off. Awkward silence descended between them.

He was botching this.

He was a wingman who needed a wingman.

He craned his neck and saw Chuck standing a couple of yards from the hors d'ouerves table.

He cleared his throat. "Did you get a chance to try the crab stuffed roll-things? I don't think I've ever tasted anything like it before."

He wasn't sure he'd liked it. He was a steak and potatoes kind of guy.

What did Amber like? He'd been so self-absorbed that he'd never noticed if she had favorites, even though she cooked for him and Bo most nights.

"I was actually thinking I might sneak away," she said. She still wasn't quite meeting his eye. "The snow isn't letting up."

He knew she didn't like driving in bad

weather. Last winter had been the only time she'd pushed back when he'd asked her to do something for Bo. She'd refused to drive on a night when they'd had some rain and the temperature had dropped below freezing.

But poor Chuck needed his chance.

And Jace wasn't sure he was ready to be under the same roof as Amber until he got rid of this crazy attraction.

"You can't leave yet." He made the mistake of putting his hand beneath her elbow, as if he was going to physically hold her in place.

Her skin was warm, soft like the afghan he'd noticed she liked to curl up with on cool evenings. She looked up at him, surprise etched on her face. Her gaze was open, searching, her eyes framed by long lashes.

He wasn't just attracted, he was ensnared...

No, he wasn't.

He dropped her arm like a hot branding iron.

Tried to make light of it. "C'mon over to the food tables"—where Chuck could intercept them —"and if the roads get bad, I'll drive you home in my truck."

Danger. Danger.

21

But her smile seemed to even out a little, and she let him usher her through the crowd.

He met Chuck's eyes over a lady's head—one of the few he didn't recognize—and widened his eyes. The guy better make this worth it. Jace was making a fool of himself.

And he hadn't even brought up Chuck yet.

When two couples blocked their winding path, he had to squeeze close to Amber. Her shoulder brushed his bicep, and for the first time, he was aware that her head would fit neatly against his shoulder if he pulled her in close.

He breathed in to try and clear his thinking, but that was a mistake because he got a whiff of something peach.

Chuck. Think about Chuck.

"So..." He didn't know how to ask without being obvious. "Are you seeing anybody? Socially, I mean. Dating. Are you dating anyone?"

She glanced at him sideways. "I only have one day off a week."

He knew that. She took care of Bo from breakfast until bedtime, though Jace had been trying his hardest this year to reserve the hours after Bo's half-day kindergarten for family time.

Was she saying she'd date if she had more

time off? She was a young woman. Maybe she wanted more free hours.

He'd never even given it a thought. What a selfish jerk.

"If you wanted—I mean, Bo and I don't need to monopolize your time. Now that winter's coming on, if you need more time off to be with your friends, or go out, you know... that can be arranged."

Had they cranked up the fireplace or something? He felt like he was sweating through his suit coat.

Awkward much?

"Oh." She was looking at the floor. Great job. "I like hanging out with Bo. And with you."

She looked up at him with those expressive eyes, and if it wouldn't have sounded cheesy, he'd have said time stopped.

Danger!

He cleared his throat again. Where the heck was Chuck?

AMBER DIDN'T KNOW whether to laugh or cry as she let Jace sweep her through the crowd.

She should've just gone home.

Jace wanted her to date other people.

At least that's what it sounded like.

Unless she was misreading his cues. Which was also possible.

It wasn't like she had a ton of experience. She'd only been on two first dates. Had never made it to a third date with either.

Her whirling thoughts stalled out when they reached the hors d'oeurves tables. They were laden with bite-sized treats, everything from bacon-wrapped asparagus to some elaborate kind of cheese on a cracker, what looked like lamb, and even the crab cake that Jace had mentioned. And then she got a look at the dessert table.

"Oh, my goodness," she whispered. "I don't even know what to try."

"Try one of everything," Jace said.

"You sound like Bo." She said the words teasingly and was rewarded with his open smile. His rare smile.

He started filling a plate.

"That's not for me, is it?" she protested as the food kept piling on.

He grinned. "We'll share it."

Did he realize how intimate that sounded?

Not like someone who wouldn't even dance with her. Yes, she was still stinging from that.

He seemed to be looking over her shoulder, and she turned her head that direction. What was he looking at?

But she only saw faces in the crowd.

When she turned back to him, Jace was smiling down at her.

They moved several paces away from the food tables and tucked in to an empty space along the wall. Outside the window, the snow seemed to be floating down even harder. Thinking about driving home in it made her stomach swoop.

I'll drive you home.

Jace couldn't know how much she wanted the words to be true. She wanted her home to be with him and Bo on the Cantrell ranch.

But it wasn't, not really. She was just the hired help.

"Can I ask why you brought up my relationship status?" she asked.

She might perish of embarrassment if he'd figured out that she'd gotten all dolled up for him.

He winced slightly. "I don't know. I guess... I

started thinking about Patricia, and then I realized maybe you had a special someone, and I've
been so self-absorbed that I never even thought
to ask."

"Oh."

Patricia. His wife.

She knew how much Patricia had meant to
both father and son. Bo talked about her often,
reminding Amber—and Jace—about some of the
special things they'd done together.

Jace rarely brought her up. But Amber had
seen him standing in the living room, staring at
the family portrait hanging on one wall. More
than once, she'd caught him there. Grieving.
Missing his wife.

Of course Jace hadn't noticed Amber. He had
a Patricia-shaped hole in his heart.

Patricia, who'd been a good wife, a great
mom. Who didn't come from the kind of mess
that Amber did.

It was no wonder he'd never noticed her,
because there was no way she could compare.

She shouldn't have even tried. Maybe if she
could choke down some of the food on this plate,
she could excuse herself and get out of here.

She took a bite of the mini-croissant. It melted on her tongue, her taste buds lighting up.

"Oh, my goodness," she gushed. "This is *so* good. It puts my cooking to shame."

"No way. You make the best baked mac 'n cheese this side of Oklahoma. With that bacon and the cheese crumbles on top... Mmm."

Her cheeks felt as hot as one of the old-style Christmas bulbs. She had to laugh and shake her head at Jace's antics, the goofy smile he wore.

"I'm serious. You've got skills. Did you learn to cook from your mom?"

"No," she said quickly. Too quickly.

Jace's brows came together. "Your grandma, then?"

"No." She tried for the brightest smile she could come up with. "Self-taught."

She'd raided the local library the first week after Jace had hired her, had borrowed ten cookbooks, and each night after Bo went to bed, had meticulously copied down recipes into a spiral notebook until her eyes had crossed.

And there'd been plenty of times she'd messed up the recipes—once she'd burned an entire pot roast. And since Jace paid for the groceries, she'd raided her meager savings to pay back the grocery fund. She'd never mentioned it to him.

She hadn't realized that getting to know Jace meant feeling like a bug under a microscope. At home, their conversations always revolved around Bo, Bo's schooling, or the next day's menu.

Jace was just being polite, making conversation. Because he didn't know about her background.

She'd done her best to make it disappear, the way she'd disappeared from her old life.

She didn't want it resurrected now, not when she was happy with her job, loved Bo.

She really didn't want Jace to feel sorry for her. Or concerned that she wasn't good for Bo.

The few bites of food she'd managed settled like lead in her stomach.

Jace exhaled, the breath so big that it stirred the fine hairs at her temple. "Look, I'm not very good at this. I have... there's this guy. A friend of mine. And he's... he'd like to ask you out on a date. At least, I think he would. He's kinda shy."

A friend.

Jace wanted to set her up with someone else.

The final fragments of hope that she'd been

holding onto crashed and broke into millions of tiny specks.

Jace wasn't interested in her at all.

Her face was on fire, and he was watching her. She couldn't look him in the eye.

"Um." She tried to smile, but her lips wobbled, and she clamped them together. "I don't know what to say." To her horror, she felt hot tears prick her eyes. She blinked rapidly. She couldn't cry in front of Jace! "I've got something in my eye." There. At least her voice hadn't broken. "Would you excuse me for a minute?"

She didn't give him time to answer, just fled, escaped down the nearest hallway. Bathroom. She needed a bathroom.

Or somewhere else to hide. Anywhere.

CHAPTER 3

JACE HAD TOTALLY SCREWED THAT UP.

He dumped the plate of half-eaten hors d'ouerves on a passing waiter's tray and spun, scanning for Chuck. He caught sight of Cash Trudeau dancing with a blonde-haired woman Jace didn't recognize.

No Chuck. Seriously, where was he? The dude was supposed to have come over and introduced himself!

Although, judging by Amber's reaction, maybe it was better that he hadn't.

I've got something in my eye.

Liar. After twelve years of marriage, he could recognize when a woman was about to cry.

But why had his words caused such a reaction? All he'd asked was whether she might be interested in going out with a friend of his.

If she wasn't interested in Chuck, no one was going to force her on a date with the guy.

But maybe it hadn't been his fumbling question.

She'd gone quiet when he'd brought up her family. He wracked his brain but couldn't think of a time he'd heard her talk about her family. Which was weird. She was great with Bo. The best. She'd have to have learned that somewhere, right? Maybe she simply wasn't close with her family.

Or maybe he was still self-absorbed. Maybe he should've offered her some time off for the holiday to be with them.

He was such a jerk.

Even more so for not going after her when he'd known she was upset. He and Patricia had had their share of fights, tears, and making up. He wasn't as scared off by a woman's tears as some of his single friends were.

He was more afraid that if he tried to comfort her, he'd end up pulling her into his arms.

Because he'd almost done just that, here in

the ballroom. He'd completely forgotten about Chuck.

The only thing that had saved him was Bo.

Bo needed Amber.

Which meant Jace needed to to keep his hands off.

Chuck appeared out of the crowd, and Jace strode up to him, not caring that they were in the middle of lots of nosy ears.

"Where the heck were you? I thought you were coming over to introduce yourself."

The other man looked intimated, and Jace reminded himself that this wasn't his business.

"I was g-going to," Chuck stammered. "But I took another look at her in that dress, and I just... I just..." He shrugged as if Jace would know what he meant.

He had no clue.

"Look," Jace said. "You just gotta gather up your courage and ask her to dance or something, okay?" Jace wanted no more part of this.

He'd hang around awhile longer. Offer Amber a ride home if she needed it. Even better, maybe he could just follow her in his truck, make sure she made it back to the ranch safely. Without being in the same vehicle.

He was a coward.

"Please," Chuck said. "I'm begging you. The last girl I had a crush on ended up marrying my best friend."

Ouch.

But still, not Jace's problem.

Chuck kept going. "If you could just talk to her one more time for me. Please. Tell her I think she's beautiful. And that I admire her."

Jace shook his head. This was over his head. He was out.

Except he couldn't quite erase the memory of her eyes filling with tears, ones she'd quickly tried to hide.

He'd messed up, somehow.

He didn't care about Chuck, one way or another. Not really.

But he needed to make things right with Amber.

For Bo's sake.

AMBER DUCKED into what must have been a guest bedroom somewhere in the back of the sprawling house.

Mansion. Just call it what it was.

A house that Amber would never be able to afford, not in her wildest dreams.

It was dark, and that was good. She didn't turn on the light.

Blinded by tears now, she stumbled over the corner of the bed and couldn't help a small cry.

"Ouch. Are you okay?"

Crap. Double crap.

That was a woman's voice. Someone was in here.

"Yeah. I'm f-fine." Her voice broke, betraying her.

But the overhead light didn't go on.

A softer light did. From an attached bathroom.

Amber was peripherally aware of the unknown woman's shoes tapping on the tiled floor, then going quiet again when she walked on the plush carpet.

A wad of tissues was pressed into her hand.

"Th-thanks," she whispered.

And then her throat was too clogged with tears to say anything else.

She sat on the end of the bed. It dipped when the mystery woman sat next to her.

She hated crying in general. Her face puffed up and turned a blotchy red.

Crying in front of anyone else... even worse.

But she couldn't seem to stop the tears. She'd put so much hope into tonight's event. Didn't she know how dangerous hope could be?

"Is there anything I can do?" the mystery woman asked.

Amber mopped at her face, even though she was still crying. "I d-don't think so." She hiccupped.

"Can I call someone for you? Your husband? Or boyfriend? Sister? Mom?"

Amber laughed through her tears, the sound slightly hysterical. "None of those."

The other woman was silent for several moments, long enough for Amber to take several deep breaths as she tried to get ahold of herself.

"I'll be all right," Amber said. Her tears were finally starting to dry up.

She'd come through worse than this rejection, hadn't she? It might hurt for now, but she wasn't going to *die*. Even if she did feel humiliated and hopeless.

"Is it man trouble?" the mystery woman asked.

Amber gave another teary laugh. "That obvious?"

She sighed. "Just a feeling. I'm having some of that kind of trouble myself."

Amber might not be acquainted with the woman sitting next to her, but she'd showed compassion and consideration, and Amber felt a little kinship with her.

"Why does it have to be so hard?" the mystery woman asked. "Actually, my situation is kind of my fault."

Amber bit her lip. Why not spill it all? It wasn't like she knew this woman. "The man I've been in love with for months just told me about a friend he wants to set me up with."

"Ouch. That sucks."

There was a beat of silence.

"Did he name this friend, or was it more like, 'I've got this friend...'" The mystery woman shifted on the bed. "Just curious."

"The latter." Amber wiped beneath her eyes with the tissue. Her tears had run dry. If she could wait another few minutes, the red blotches on her face might fade enough that she could sneak back through the ballroom and make her escape.

"I don't know your situation," mystery woman said, "but maybe your guy was talking about himself."

"What?" That sounded a little out there to Amber.

"Is there any reason he might not want to come on too strong?"

Amber considered. "I'm his son's nanny."

"Aha." Mystery woman sounded way more upbeat than Amber could muster. "Maybe he wanted to broach the idea without you knowing it was him, to feel things out. Then if you said no, it wasn't an outright rejection."

Are you seeing anybody? Socially, I mean. Dating. Are you dating anyone? Jace's fumbling words replayed in her memory.

And the tiny kernel of the hope that had died so spectacularly came back to life.

"I don't know," Amber said slowly. "I mean, he did ask me if I was dating anyone. But then he told me about this friend of his. Who was shy."

It was weird.

Jace wasn't usually someone to beat around the bush. When it came to Bo, he was quick to let her know what his son needed and how things should be done. If he was going to be out in the barn late, he called and told her. He didn't waste a lot of time hemming and hawing.

But... "He's a widower," she said softly.

"So, there you go," Mystery woman said. "Maybe he was uncomfortable just coming right out and asking you out."

Could she be right?

Amber's hope swelled, but she was a little afraid to trust it. What if she was wrong?

"There's only one way to find out," Mystery woman said. "Ask him outright."

Amber could never do that. She'd spent the money on her dress, hair, and makeup, hoping Jace would notice her. Asking him out on a date? She lived in his house. If she was wrong, there would be humiliation involved. Every day. It was too risky. Wasn't it?

"I should go home," she said. "I'm pretty sure my makeup is ruined."

"Oh, I can fix that."

Maybe her heart wasn't broken after all, because it pulsed painfully as she let her mystery friend pull her into the well-appointed bathroom.

Under the bright bathroom lights, she winced at her image in the mirror, the one with mascara running down both cheeks. The puffiness beneath her eyes had diminished some, but the tip of her nose was still bright red.

She got her first good look at her new friend as the other woman rummaged in a medium-sized purse. She wore a black cocktail dress, and her blond hair was pulled back in a simple updo. She had compassionate eyes. "Here we go." She handed Amber a packet of makeup wipes. "Those babies will take anything off."

Amber hesitated before taking them. "I don't even know your name."

"I'm Delaney." The other woman had a warm smile, one that Amber found herself returning.

"I'm Amber. Nice to meet you."

Maybe Delaney was right.

Maybe she did still have a chance with Jace.

She leaned over the counter as she used the makeup wipe beneath her eyes. By the time she'd scrubbed away the smeared mascara, her foundation had come away too, leaving weird patches on her cheeks. She sighed and began scrubbing at her entire face.

The makeup hadn't really been *her*. The makeup artist from Austin had caked it on, while Amber usually chose a more natural look. She'd thought it made her look striking, but maybe all those looks in the ballroom were folks thinking she shouldn't be trying so hard.

"Our skin tones aren't a match, but I think I can fix your eye makeup."

Amber blinked at her bare face in the mirror. Without the mascara and the smoky way her eyes had been made up, she was just... Amber.

For better or for worse.

"I think I'll just go like this." Jace was used to seeing her first thing in the morning, messy hair bun and no makeup as she got Bo ready for the early bus. If he was interested in her, the makeup wouldn't matter. Right?

"I've taken up too much of your night," she continued. "You're missing the party."

For the first time, Delaney grimaced. "Yeah." It was her turn to sigh. "I'm not exactly on the guest list." What did that mean? "And not being on the guest list is why I'm having man troubles."

Amber shook her head, confused.

But Delaney just gave her a gentle push toward the door. "Don't worry about me. You go get your guy."

Amber's stomach was jumping as if a whole flock of Christmas geese had taken up residence there. But she obediently made her way out of the darkened bedroom.

She was going to do this.

She was going to ask Jace if he'd meant *he* was the friend.

CHAPTER 4

"This is stupid," Amber whispered to herself as she rejoined the crowd in the ballroom.

The momentary confidence she'd felt as a result of Delaney's encouragement was fast dwindling.

If Jace wanted to ask her out, he'd just do it. Wouldn't he?

She shouldn't do this. She was just setting herself up for heartbreak. And probably risking her job. She would hate it if she got fired and never got to see Bo again.

Guys like Jace weren't interested in girls like her. Were they?

She let her gaze roam the ballroom. It bounced off a brown-haired guy standing near the tree, halfway across the room. His eyes met hers, but then he quickly glanced away.

There was Jace. Adjacent to her, standing close to the part of the room reserved for the dance floor.

He seemed to be scanning the room, too. When his gaze landed on her, a look of determination crossed his features.

What was that about?

He began making his way toward her, skirting other couples as he edged around the dance floor.

Her heart was pounding now, her pulse drumming in her ears.

She moved to meet him.

Except she didn't calculate that they'd meet right in front of the string quartet, which was playing beautiful Christmas music—currently *Santa Claus is Coming to Town*—but this close, it was impossibly loud.

"Are you okay?" She saw more than heard his words.

It was impossible not to blush under his intent gaze. She nodded. Gathered up her courage.

"Do you want—?"

"Listen, there's—"

She saw his lips move at the same time she'd started to ask if he'd go on a date with her.

He grimaced, tilted his head toward the band. Mouthed *it's loud*.

"Do you want to dance?" he asked.

Her heart went into double time even as she panicked. She didn't know how. She nodded before she'd thought better of it.

And just as they merged with the couples on the dance floor, just as Jace took her hand, the tune changed. To *I'll Be Home for Christmas*. A slow version.

Which meant a slow dance.

In the microsecond as he turned to face her, Jace looked extremely uncomfortable. His expression cleared, and he carefully took her in his arms. One hand at her waist, the other clasped between them.

With a respectable amount of distance between them.

It might not be as close as she'd like, but he was holding her.

"I've never done this before," she confessed softly.

"Never?" His eyebrows lifted. "No high school dances?"

She shook her head, feeling a blush rising. Her high school experience had been atypical— and she'd never been invited to a dance. Wouldn't have been able to go if she had.

His gaze softened as gazed down at her.

What if she bumped into someone? Or worse? "What if I step on your feet?"

"Can't be worse than a heifer stomping on me. Just follow my lead."

His smile was warm. Had she imagined the discomfort that had crossed his face moments ago?

Being in his arms like this felt right. Like she belonged.

She was a little afraid her heart was shining through her eyes. She focused on a point over his shoulder.

"It was a little too loud to talk over there," he said.

She nodded. *Say something.*

"Do you—?"

He spoke over her. "About before. I'm sorry if I said anything wrong. I hadn't thought about—

should I have given you some time off to visit your family for the holidays?"

She missed a step, faltering in his arms. His hold broke slightly until he reclaimed her waist, holding her slightly closer this time.

"I don't see my family—that is, I don't really have family to see." She stumbled over her words, hating the fact that hot color was flaring into her face again.

She dared a glance at his face. He was watching her, concern etched on his features. He mumbled something that sounded like, "I really have been a selfish jerk."

What? He was one of the least selfish people she knew. If he wasn't working on the ranch, he was being a dad to Bo.

"If you told me when you first came to us, I don't remember," he said. "Where are you from? What's your family like?"

She didn't know what to do with his sudden interest. Was it the holidays making him think about it?

Or was he worried about her influence on Bo? Had he somehow figured her secret out, even though she'd kept it since she'd arrived in Sawyer Creek?

"I'm from a little town in Oklahoma," she said carefully. "I haven't been back there since I turned eighteen."

She didn't want to lie to him—wouldn't lie if he asked outright, but she really didn't want to talk about family.

"Do you want to..." She lost her nerve halfway through the question. "Can you tell me more about this friend you mentioned? The shy one?"

Heat flared even higher.

This time he missed a step, and since they were closer now, his boot nudged her shoe. "Sorry," he mumbled.

That was definitely discomfort she saw in his expression.

"Well, he's... a rancher. He's lived in Sawyer Creek for years."

That was good. Both of those could identify Jace himself. Maybe Delaney was right.

"I don't know if you'd call him handsome or not, but he's a good guy. Goes to church and all that."

Oh, she did find him handsome.

She bit her lower lip, trying desperately to contain the joyful smile that was bubbling up.

"And what about his family? Does he have kids?" she dared to ask.

Jace's brows pinched. "Uh, no. I think he has a niece."

A niece.

Not a son.

The joy and hope that had been blossoming within wilted. Oh, my goodness. How humiliating.

"You mean, you really do have a friend?"

THIS WAS his stupidest idea yet.

Having Amber in his arms was equal parts heaven and hell. She fit *perfectly*, like she was made for him. She'd scrubbed her face clean of the makeup she'd been wearing earlier. She looked like the girl next door. She smelled so good, and he fought the desire to pull her closer.

His senses were muddled. She'd asked him about Chuck, and he'd told her, but now there was no missing her sudden tension. *You really do have a friend?*

"Yeah," he said, aware that he was suddenly wading through a minefield with no map. "His name is Chuck."

She stepped out of his arms, a discordant move in the melody of their dance.

"Oh." Both of her hands came up to cover her cheeks. "This is—" Her eyes darted away. She looked anything but happy, even though moments before she'd been shining up at him.

Luckily they were close enough to the edge of the dance floor that they were out of the flow of traffic.

"This is really embarrassing," she said.

He didn't get it.

And then his phone rang from his breast pocket. He'd turned the volume up so he'd be able to hear it over the party noise. He still wasn't that comfortable leaving Bo with a babysitter.

He pulled it from his pocket, hoping that Amber would forgive him for interrupting their conversation.

"It's Mrs. Ritter," he said, flashing her a glimpse of the screen.

Her expression shifted to worry. He started toward the front entry even as he answered, putting the phone to his ear. "Cantrell."

He glanced over his shoulder. Amber was right behind him.

At first, he couldn't hear Mrs. Ritter over the

noise of the crowd, but as the crowd thinned, her voice came through.

"...having some kind of reaction."

His body felt cleaved in two. "What do you mean *reaction*?"

The foyer was completely empty except for the dark-suited attendant who'd taken his coat earlier.

He turned wildly, and Amber was right there.

"He's got these red spots across his stomach. Some kind of rash—"

He spoke to Amber. "A rash on his stomach. Red spots."

Panic rose. Was Bo having an allergic reaction? Should he have Mrs. Ritter call 911?

Amber's hand on his forearm steadied him out of the boiling panic.

"How big are the spots? How long since he ate anything?" Amber whispered.

"I've got Amber here, too," he told Mrs. Ritter. "She wants to know how big are the spots and how long since he ate anything?"

He closed his eyes for a moment, thankful that Amber was here to be the voice of reason. She knew Bo just as intimately as he did.

Mrs. Ritter was rattling in his ear and he realized he hadn't heard any of it.

He took a deep breath, moved the phone away from his ear, and put it on speaker.

"Mrs. Ritter, can you say that last part again? I've got you on speaker now."

"The spots start out small but they've spread across his sides and on his back. He ate his dinner at six, just like you said."

Amber was close to his side, her hand still on his forearm, though she didn't seem to notice. "Is he having any trouble breathing? Any fever?"

He glanced at Amber again, because he wouldn't have even thought to ask either of those things.

"No fever. He's breathing just fine."

Amber exhaled noisily and squeezed his arm. "That's good."

"Should we call 911?" he asked her, because he didn't want to make this decision on his own. "Take him to the hospital?"

She shook her head. "Let's call the nurse line and see if it's okay to give him some Benadryl. We can do that on the way home."

"Mrs. Ritter, we're coming to you," he said into the phone. They rang off.

LACY WILLIAMS

The coat attendant retrieved their coats. Amber's hand jingled in her pocket as they stepped onto the front porch together.

The world was buried in white. Snow was falling in crazy swirls.

Amber's face had paled to the color of the drifting snow.

He put his hand under her elbow. "I'll drive. We can come back for your car tomorrow."

She sent him a grateful glance that was quickly shadowed by something else.

This is so embarrassing.

The untimely phone call had interrupted their conversation on the dance floor. He'd stepped wrong, and he didn't mean the dance moves that had been aborted.

Amber tucked her face into the collar of her coat, her shoulders hunched against the cold that crept in the back of his jacket and down his spine.

A part of him wanted to throw his arm over her shoulders and tuck her close. Protect her. Keep her warm.

The caveman-like impulse surprised him. What he'd felt when he'd seen her in the ballroom was a visceral attraction. This was something more.

This is so embarrassing.

Why should she be embarrassed that Chuck was interested in her?

The windshield of his truck was covered in snow, the wipers frozen to the window. Snow had accumulated in little mountains around each of his tires.

Her feet had to be freezing in those fancy shoes. And that dress. He opened her door and didn't wait for an invitation before he cupped her waist in both hands and boosted her up. It was too cold to be polite.

He shut the door and rounded his truck to get in the driver's side, knocking snow off his boots quickly before he got in.

He turned over the engine, cranking up the heat even though it wouldn't warm up for minutes.

Did they have minutes to spare?

Amber was dialing her cell phone as he reached across and opened the glove compartment for his ice scraper. His hand bumped her knee, and she jumped.

She put the phone to her ear, pretending she hadn't noticed.

But he knew she had.

"Can I have the pediatric on-call nurse, please?" she said into the phone.

She was taking care of his son.

Hot emotion boiled in his chest as he backed out of the truck to scrape what he could off the windshield.

He'd forgotten what it felt like to be part of a team. He didn't have to worry alone tonight because Amber was here.

What would it be like if Amber were taking care of *him*?

THEY WERE halfway home before Amber got off the phone with the on-call nurse.

She made a quick call to Mrs. Ritter to tell her the dosage of Benadryl.

And then there was nothing but silence in the cab of Jace's truck.

She wished the call had gone on longer.

Jace hadn't been trying to feel her out. He wasn't interested. He wanted to set her up with his friend.

A new wave of humiliation pummeled her. Stupid. Stupid. Stupid.

At least now she had something else to focus on. Bo. She was worried about the boy, wouldn't feel better until she saw for himself that he was all right.

Caring for Bo was the best job she'd ever had. She'd put down roots in Sawyer Creek. She'd been so blessed to find the work. And being Bo's nanny would be enough for her.

It was wrong to wish for more.

The quiet in the cab was broken when Jace cleared his throat. "What'd you mean back there, in the ballroom?"

Oh, crap. Really? He couldn't just be a gentleman and let it go?

She didn't answer, kept her eyes on the snow swirling outside the window. Jace was going maybe ten miles an hour, and that felt fast in this roaring storm. But they needed to get back to Bo.

"Amber?"

Heat prickled in her cheeks. Hopefully, he was too focused on driving to notice.

"I don't know what you mean," she said to the window.

"You said you felt embarrassed."

Seriously? The man was like a dog with a bone.

She let one of her hands pass over her eyes. Grabbed for a straw. "We should focus on Bo, shouldn't we?"

There was a beat of silence between them. "It'll be at least ten minutes before we hit the driveway."

Yeah, but she didn't want to humiliate herself any more than she already had.

"Did I say something that embarrassed you?"

"Oh, my gosh!" she blurted. "Double gosh. You can't leave it alone, can you? I'm embarrassed because when you said you had a friend, I thought you meant yourself. I thought *you* wanted to ask me out. Are you happy now?"

She framed her eyes with both hands, too ashamed to look at him after that outburst.

And then he didn't say anything.

And still didn't say anything.

She pressed her palms against her eyes. "Can we please just forget about this whole night?"

The heater kicked to a lower setting, not burning her bare legs quite so badly.

Was Jace... chuckling?

She turned her head, still half-hiding her face behind her fingers.

He was laughing, drawing one hand down his face. He didn't look particularly happy.

"I messed things up completely," he said. "Bumbled my way through like a seventh grader. It's no wonder you were confused."

He sighed. "I'm sorry to have embarrassed you. I should've told Chuck to do his own courting. He is a nice guy, but—you don't think I'm too old for you?" he asked suddenly.

Nothing he'd said indicated he was interested in her. Just sorry that she'd been embarrassed.

She turned her face back to the front, kept her eyes and burning cheeks covered. "I'm twenty-four. You're only six years older."

"You're twenty-four?"

"Don't sound so incredulous," she snapped. She wished to be out of this truck. Wished the night was over. Wished she could sink through the ground.

"I'm sorry," he said quickly. "You just don't look twenty-four. In a good way."

She was too resigned to even care. How many times in one night could a guy tell you he wasn't interested?

The tires crunched on the familiar gravel drive, even through the snow. Thank goodness. They were home. She could check on Bo and then hide in her room. Forever.

The truck rolled to a stop.

"Amber, I..."

Jace's hesitant start made her pause when she would've jumped out of the truck—before he'd even thrown it in Park. Her hand closed over the cool door handle.

"I haven't even thought about dating anybody since Patricia died."

Hot emotion rose in her throat in a knot. She nodded. Of course he hadn't.

"We should go in," she whispered, throat tight. Ten more minutes. Thirty at the most, and she could hide away and lick her wounds.

"Wait for me, the porch steps are always slick."

She heard his words but already had the truck door open and her feet on the ground.

She didn't want to wait, didn't want him to see how near tears she was. Again.

Stupid.

She crossed the yard, snow getting between

her toes in the fancy, not-ranch-appropriate heels she'd worn to the party.

She'd just hold onto the wooden railing.

Except it was covered in an inch of snow that bit into her hand.

She could sense Jace coming up behind her. One hand rested at her waist as she took the second stair. It was slick, but not too bad.

She turned to tell him so—

And her heel caught in a crack between two wooden boards.

She pitched forward, but he was there. Before she hit her hands and knees on the porch, he'd caught her with both arms around her waist.

Pulled her back upright.

She was too close, standing almost chest-to-chest.

She was too humiliated to look him full in the face.

But—

"Amber..." His voice was a near-groan.

And then he was pulling her even closer, one hand moving to bury itself in her hair.

His lips crashed down on hers. His kiss was both fierce and gentle. His hand on her hip was possessive.

And she never wanted him to let go.

But snow was melting between her toes, and she couldn't help the full-body shiver that wracked her.

He pulled away, eyes wide and nostrils flaring with emotion.

"I didn't mean—"

To do that.

He didn't get the words out before the door opened, a block of light spilling onto the porch and illuminating them.

"Dad! Amber! You're home."

CHAPTER 5

JACE STRODE INSIDE AND SCOOPED THE PAJAMA-
clad boy into his arms.

Emotion clenched his chest like a saddle cinch drawn too tight. His son was all right. At least, he seemed to be.

Jace was acutely aware of Amber stepping into the entryway behind him, closing the door.

That kiss!

Bo pounded on his shoulder. "Put me down. I want Amber!"

Yeah, get in line, son.

Jace set Bo on his feet. The boy bounced—bounced!—to his nanny.

Amber gathered his son into her arms. Her eyes closed as she held him close, and Jace recognized, not for the first time, how deeply she cared.

"You scared us," Amber said, still holding the boy. She set Bo away from her. "Show me your tummy."

Bo proudly pulled his shirt up high enough that he covered his face.

From where he stood, Jace could see small red splotches up and down Bo's back.

Amber ran one hand down Bo's tummy. "Does it itch?"

"Nu-uh." Bo dropped his shirt and bounced again.

It was well after his bedtime. Where was this energy coming from?

"Can I have a snack? I'm hungry."

Amber ruffled Bo's hair. "You're always hungry."

"Just like Daddy!" Bo chimed, glancing over his shoulder at Jace.

Jace met Amber's eyes over the boy's head. She'd responded to his kiss, and just remembering it now was tightening his gut.

Yes, he was hungry. For Amber.

She looked away quickly, color climbing into her cheeks.

This night hadn't turned out anything like he'd thought. He'd expected the boring old Cattlemen's Ball. Had gone into it with all the enthusiasm of the Grinch. And now he was thinking things he definitely shouldn't be about his son's nanny.

Mrs. Ritter bustled out of the kitchen, already bundling herself into a thick parka, her purse over one arm. "I'm sorry to cut and run, but have you seen that snow out there? I've got to make it home before"—she caught herself and smiled down at Bo—"before Santa gets here."

Jace followed her out the front door, taking her arm to help her down the steps.

He quizzed her about Bo.

When she had her hand on the door of her 4x4 SUV, she turned to him. "Look. I'd put him in bed like you said. I was watching TV. All of a sudden, he was standing in the door. When I put him back in bed, his shirt rode up, and I saw the spots. That's when I called you."

She pulled open the door without waiting for him to say anything else. It *was* snowing, maybe even harder than before. Not the best conditions for a chat.

But something about the way her eyes had

shifted told Jace that maybe she hadn't given him all of the story.

As a babysitter, she'd come highly recommended by a friend. Maybe he was paranoid, but he sensed something was off.

He rubbed one hand over his face as he carefully trudged up the porch steps and back into the house.

He should head out to the barn, make sure his stock was tucked in for the night, and check on the neighbor's visiting puppies.

But worry for Bo won out. He'd make sure his son was all right first.

In the foyer, he took off his overcoat and hung it in the coat closet. In the living room, he shed the tuxedo jacket and his boots, then searched for his son in his shirtsleeves and socks.

Bo and Amber were in the brightly-lit kitchen. Bo sat at the table, his feet swinging back and forth above the floor.

Amber was at the stove, assembling what looked like a grilled cheese sandwich.

She'd taken off her coat—it hung over one of the empty kitchen chairs—leaving him to gaze at her in in those heels and that killer dress.

"...sometimes I get the munchies when I take

medicine too," she was saying over her shoulder to Bo.

He remembered the shiver that had gone through her when he'd held her close. It was nice and toasty in the house, but surely she'd like a chance to warm up.

He came up behind her, reached out to touch her shoulder. "Amber—"

Her skin was a soft as a baby kitten, but she jumped beneath his touch.

"Hey," he held both hands in front of him. "Thought you might want to change out of that dress. Get warmed up. I think I can handle a grilled cheese."

"Fine." She didn't meet his eyes as she quickly ducked down the hallway toward her bedroom at the back of the house.

Crap. He'd messed everything up because he couldn't keep his lips to himself. He hadn't spared one thought for Chuck. Or Bo.

He had no idea what he was doing.

Except making a sandwich. He could make a sandwich. And one for himself, because the hors d'ouerves he'd consumed at the party suddenly weren't enough.

"Mrs. Ritter said you got out of bed. Were you feeling sick?"

He stuck the last piece of bread on top and turned to check on Bo.

The boy was standing on top of the table, reaching for the overhead light fixture.

"Bo!" Jace lunged and grabbed his son by the waist, then set him back in the chair. "Why do you have so much energy?"

Bo wiggled in the chair but stayed seated. He shrugged. "I dunno."

Jace put on his Dad Face. "Did you get out of bed because you felt sick?"

Bo shrugged again, his eyes downcast. "Sorta."

Amber returned, watching from the doorway. She'd put on red pajama pants with reindeer hoofprints on them—at least he supposed that's what they were—and an oversize T-shirt. Her hair was down around her shoulders, her face scrubbed free of makeup. She had been wearing makeup, hadn't she?

She looked nothing like the glamorous woman in the hot dress.

So his attraction should've waned.

But it didn't.

He wanted to go to her, draw her into his arms again.

It was as if he'd seen her for the first time. And now he couldn't un-see the beautiful woman she was.

She again avoided his eyes as she entered the room.

She went to the stove and flipped the grilled cheese sandwiches as he sat on the edge of the seat across from Bo.

"Did you sneak into the pantry while Mrs. Ritter was watching TV?" Amber asked from the stove.

Bo shook his head, but Amber glanced over her shoulder, finally meeting Jace's eyes. She shook her head slightly.

She didn't believe Bo either.

AMBER WANTED nothing more than to retreat to her bedroom. The clock was edging toward midnight, but she didn't expect any Christmas goodies from Santa.

Right now she'd settle for a magic potion that would make Jace forget the events that had transpired tonight.

Especially the kiss.

It had been everything Amber had dreamed of. Until the moment Jace had pulled away.

The look on his face...

He'd been terrified. Of kissing her.

She just wanted to go to bed, but Bo was wound up. Plus, she wanted to make sure the rash was fading and not getting worse.

"Bo..." Jace's voice held a hint of warning to it.

"Maybe I came to the kitchen and got a snack first," the boy said, head hanging low.

"How come Mrs. Ritter didn't see you?" Amber asked.

Jace went to the pantry and opened the cabinet door.

"I army-crawled past the living room," Bo said. "And kept the light off in the kitchen."

Army crawled. Boys.

Amber had never been a nanny before this job, hadn't spent much time around little kids, and Bo's antics had often surprised her in the beginning. Not so much anymore. He'd been hungry.

"What'd you eat?" she asked.

"I think I can answer that," Jace said. When he

turned, he had a half-empty bag of corn nuts in his hand.

"And you're still hungry?" Amber said.

Bo nodded exaggeratedly.

Amber slid the sandwiches on paper plates she pulled from the cabinet above the stove. No use getting more dishes dirty this late.

She took Bo's sandwich to the table, taking time to hug the boy's shoulders before she sat in the adjacent chair.

Jace leaned his hips against the counter, munching on his sandwich where he stood. She could barely look at him. Even in his sock feet, with the collar of his shirt open, he was easily the sexiest man she'd ever known. His evening scruff had come in, making a dark shadow on his jaw.

Now she knew how that jaw felt under her fingers.

She cut her eyes to the tabletop. That was not a safe line of thinking.

Bo was stuffing his face. "C'n we watch a"—he gulped—"Christmas movie? What about that one with the green guy whose heart was too small?"

"Not tonight, buddy," Jace said. "Did you forget it's Christmas Eve?" He glanced at the clock. "Barely."

"But, Daaaadd."

"Remember, Santa can't come until you're asleep in bed," Amber said.

"Yeah," Bo sounded dejected as he kicked the table's center post. Then he jumped up from his chair and started bounding around the kitchen, jumping every third step. "Tomorrow's Christmas! Tomorrow's Christmas!"

She caught Jace's concerned glance.

"Should he be this energetic after having the Benadryl?" Jace asked. "That stuff usually knocks me out."

She'd been wondering the same thing. "Do you want me to call the nurse line back? Make sure nothing else is wrong?"

He grimaced. "I can do it. It's supposed to be your night off."

Bo ran toward her and slammed into her stomach with an "oof!" His arms wrapped around her in a hug.

She nuzzled her face into his hair. He smelled like kid shampoo and boy-sweat.

"I'll do it," she told Jace without looking at him. "You try and wrangle this guy back into bed."

She dialed her cell phone as Jace hauled his

son over his shoulder. Bo laughed, pounding on his dad's back.

Amber forced herself to concentrate on the automated prompts that would get her to the on-call nurse.

Seeing Jace and Bo together, playful and loving and ornery, always made her ache for the childhood she hadn't had.

And for the family she wanted to be a part of. A real part.

When she ended the call, murmured voices from the living room drew her in that direction.

The living room had been the first draw to this job—before she'd even met Bo, before she'd found out what Jace was like as a father. She'd sat on the couch with its afghan folded neatly across the headrest... and she'd wanted. Wanted to be a part of the household that left Legos strewn across the living room floor. The wall was covered in family pictures and knick-knacks. It had felt like home.

Now she glanced into the room.

Both father and son were tucked on the couch under that same afghan. A Christmas movie was playing after all, though she knew *The*

Grinch was less than an hour without commercials.

Bo's eyes were glued to the TV, but Jace glanced up at her, a chagrined smile crossing his lips. *I gave in*, he mouthed.

She couldn't help a return smile. "The nurse said that Benadryl causes some kids to have a lot of energy. She didn't think there was anything to worry about, as long as there are no other symptoms that pop up."

Jace nodded. "Thank you. For being here tonight. For knowing to call that line."

"Taking care of Bo is my job."

Her throat closed up as she pushed the words out. It was true. Taking care of Bo *was* her job.

But she also loved the boy as if he were her own son.

She edged away, toward the hall.

Everything was okay now. Jace was tucked-in on the couch with Bo.

She could go to bed.

Except Bo chose that moment to look away from the TV.

"Amber, snuggle with us!"

"Oh, no."

Bo stuck out his lower lip. "Please! Pretty

please with whipped cream and a cherry and sprinkles on top. I need your snuggles."

Oh, she loved this boy.

But she was also aware of the man sitting beside him, aware of the intent stare he was giving her. One that she couldn't quite meet and didn't know how to decipher.

She focused on Bo again. "Honey, I—"

"There's plenty of room," Jace said quietly. "Unless you're too tired."

"Yeah, there's plenty of room!" Bo echoed.

How could she say no to the pair of them?

Her heart pounded as she rounded the couch so that Bo was between her and Jace. Bo lifted the blanket, and she snuggled in until her shoulder was pressed against the boy's.

She propped her sock feet on the coffee table. Jace's were there too, a foot of open space between them.

With the overhead lights off, only the colorful lights of the Christmas tree and the TV screen illuminated the room. A window stretched long next to the TV and, because the blinds hadn't been pulled, reflected the room back to them.

Her eyes lingered there instead of on the TV.

Was Jace... watching her? His head was turned so that he was looking over Bo's head.

But he might just be staring into space.

She felt the couch move when the man shifted slightly. Then again, a few minutes later.

"Oh, I love this part!" Bo cried. On the TV screen, the Grinch was sneaking into The Whos' houses and stealing all of their Christmases.

Jace ruffled his son's hair. "You've got to try harder to fall asleep."

Bo murmured something unintelligible.

And instead of returning his hand to his lap or something, Jace stretched his arm over the back of the couch so that his fingers brushed her shoulder.

It was just happenstance.

She stared at the reflection. She was too far away to make out Jace's expression in the blurry reflection.

And then he shifted again, and his toe nudged hers.

Surprised, she couldn't help the turn of her chin toward him.

He was staring at her, considering her. His eyes were warm.

Her belly dipped as if she were riding on a

rollercoaster.

His index finger traced a small pattern on her shoulder. Even through her T-shirt, she felt burned by his touch.

She couldn't hold his gaze for long. What was he looking for?

She was so confused.

But as her lashes fluttered down, as she started to turn her chin, his finger moved to touch her jaw. She froze.

Her gaze flicked back to his.

Don't turn away, he mouthed.

Heat flooded her cheeks. Why? Was there anything left to say?

Are you sorry? she mouthed in return. For the kiss. He had to know what she meant. Her stomach tightened into a tiny ball as she waited for his answer.

His eyes softened slightly. *No.*

Her pulse began to pound in her ears.

His toes pressed against hers. An unexpectedly tender touch.

We should talk, he mouthed.

Her stomach swooped again.

And Bo's head lolled on her shoulder.

He was finally asleep.

CHAPTER 6

JACE HAD THE WORST TIMING EVER. HE NOT ONLY had no game, he had negative game.

Which is why the woman he couldn't get out of his head had to ask whether he regretted kissing her.

It was late. The clock had gone past midnight.

But there was a part of him that was afraid that whatever was happening between them would be just a dream if he let things go until the morning.

He carefully untangled himself from the blanket and stood.

"I have to get him in bed," he whispered. Bo had finally succumbed to sleep and heaven knew, he'd be up at the crack of dawn. Christmas did that.

"Will you wait for me?" he asked.

She looked a little like a frightened deer in too-bright headlights. But she nodded.

He scooped Bo into his arms, blanket and all. He'd tuck him in with the afghan as long as the boy would stay asleep.

Bo murmured, turned his head, and tucked it beneath Jace's chin. But miraculously, stayed asleep as Jace traversed the squeaky floorboards in the old farmhouse.

The nightlight was on in his son's room, giving Jace enough light to gently lay the boy on the bed. He ended up pulling the afghan off and tucking Bo's Ninja Turtle bedspread over him.

Then he stood looking down at his son.

What was he doing? With Amber.

She was an amazing woman. He knew, because she cared so much about Bo.

If he and Amber started a romantic relationship and things went sour, Bo would likely lose the one woman who'd been a steady presence in his life since Patricia had passed.

Was it worth risking that, just because Jace was attracted to her?

On the other hand... just how long would Amber be content to stay on as Bo's nanny? Next year, when he went to first grade, Bo would be in school all day long. She might get bored. Start thinking about other jobs she might like better. Or find another family to care for. Or find a man to make a family with of her own.

He didn't want Bo to lose Amber, but what if he did nothing, and she walked out of their lives anyway?

Certain that Bo was down for the count, he brushed a kiss across the boy's forehead. He loved this little guy.

He and Patricia had planned on a houseful of kids.

Did Amber want kids of her own?

On the heels of that errant thought, he slipped down the hall. This was crazy. Before tonight, he'd barely noticed that Amber was a woman. Now he was thinking about marriage. Kids. With her.

But somehow, the thought wasn't as frightening as it should've been.

He stalled in the hallway, watching Amber before she noticed he was there.

She stood in front of the rocking chair in the corner, looking down at something sitting on the back of it. She reached out to touch it, and he remembered he'd left the bow tie there. The one he hadn't been able to tie.

She picked it up, ran the silk through her fingers.

He stepped into the room, and she jumped, quickly putting the tie back where it'd been.

He gestured to it. "I couldn't remember how to tie the stupid thing," he said.

She looked a little lost.

"Patricia always tied it for me." He stepped behind the couch. With the couch and coffee table between them, maybe he'd have enough space to keep his head clear. He cleared his throat. "I was putting it on tonight and fumbling with it and, somehow, I just couldn't do it."

Some indefinable pain passed over her expression. She glanced briefly at the wall—no, the picture—behind her, then away.

The family portrait he often stared at when he felt lost. Last time, it'd been at the loss of two baby calves early in the season. He'd always shared those losses with Patricia, and it was silly to think he could find comfort from a painting, but it was something.

"I should've YouTubed it," he blurted, because he didn't want Patricia between them, not now.

"Or asked you to tie it for me." Though she'd been gone for the afternoon, appearing at the party like Cinderella or something.

"I don't know how to tie a bow tie, either." She smiled, but there was something sad in it. "I'm not"—she gestured to the portrait. "I'm not like Patricia."

Screw the distance between them. He rounded the couch in a few strides.

He reached for her, because he couldn't help it. "I don't want you to be. It's *you* I can't stop thinking about."

Maybe it was selfish, but he'd already admitted to being a self-centered jerk. He couldn't *not* kiss her again.

But he also didn't want to take away her choice.

He let one hand slide along her jaw. Slowly, savoring the moment. The fingers of his other hand buried themselves in the hair behind her head. He tipped her face up.

Her eyes were shadowed. Haunted, maybe. Was that because she believed he expected her to be like Patricia?

He leaned in slowly. If she wanted to refuse his kiss, push him away, he'd obey.

But she didn't.

"I see you," he whispered, just before he brushed a kiss to her lips.

He pulled back slightly.

"I'm kissing Amber," he whispered before he plundered her mouth.

She tasted like Christmas. Like peppermint candy canes and hot chocolate and something indefinable that was just Amber.

He didn't want to stop kissing her, but he made himself pull away. Put a foot of distance between them.

They needed to talk.

Except he looked at her, saw her wide eyes, dazzled expression, the lips he'd kissed pink and plump.

And he reeled her back in. Took her mouth again.

She responded again, kissing him back hungrily. Her fingers clutched the back of his shirt.

He could fall for her so easily...

Some dormant sense of self-preservation roared to life, and he ended the kiss. He stepped back a good yard this time, shoved his hands in his trouser pockets.

"I'm an idiot," he said.

She flinched.

"Strike that," he went on quickly. "I've been blind. It took that fantastic dress for me to notice you—and now I can't seem to figure out how I've missed that you..."

He didn't know how to say it.

She was here. A part of their lives, his and Bo's. She was important.

She was Amber.

AMBER FELT giddy and delirious from Jace's kisses.

And his words...

She'd waited so long. *Dreamed* that he would finally notice her.

But he also looked conflicted.

He took one hand out of his pocket and ran it through his hair. Hair that was already mussed. Had she done that, when she'd kissed him? She hadn't realized.

"Look, I don't want you to feel pressured," he said. "We live under the same roof. If you're not interested—"

"I am," she said quickly. Too quickly. A sudden

bout of shyness overtook her, and she looked down as heat filled her face. "I've been... interested for a long time." She'd almost blurted out *in love with you*.

Wouldn't that be fine. Making a declaration like that when he was just now noticing she was alive.

"You have," he repeated the words, not really a question. Almost a half-laugh. As if he couldn't believe her. His lips moved, but she didn't hear the word he said. Maybe "blind."

"I really want to kiss you again," he said.

Her heart leapt at the honest confession. At the heat in his eyes. For her!

But he was still over there, and now he'd shoved both hands in his pockets.

"But I'm afraid if I do, I'll forget all about assembling Bo's new bike. And I need to go check on the animals in the barn."

Oh, my goodness. For a while there, she'd forgotten the clock had chimed, turning the day over to Christmas. She had gifts to put under the tree.

"Can I help?" she asked, still unable to shake the sudden shyness that Jace's kisses had instilled.

"As long as you promise only to distract me a little bit."

Heat flooded her face.

He groaned. "And if you keep blushing like that, I'm going to *have* to kiss you again."

She pressed both hands against her burning cheeks.

Jace strode to her and gently pulled both wrists away down. He laced their fingers together. Brushed one gentle kiss across her lips. Leaned his forehead on hers. "There's a huge part of me that wants to run with this. But I think we have to be smart about it. We're not the only ones to consider, right?"

Of course. It was right that he'd be thinking about Bo, too.

"Can we take things a day at a time?" he asked.

She nodded, bumping his forehead, and then giggled like a schoolgirl. She pressed her hand against her mouth to stifle the embarrassing sound.

She just couldn't contain her joy.

Jace wanted to be with her.

He squeezed her hand. "I'm going to the barn to get that bike."

But he didn't move.

He kissed her instead.

A few breathless moments later, she asked, "Are you sure it's safe?" Because she was fairly sure the snow was still coming down outside. She couldn't seem to look away from Jace's dear face.

"I've got a line tied from the house to the barn," he murmured.

And kissed her again.

He was only holding her hands, not touching her anywhere else, but she felt lost in his kiss.

And she didn't want to be found. Ever again.

Another breathless few moments later, and he pulled away, dropping her hands and backing up until he was out of touching distance.

"I'm going to the barn."

He ran a hand through his hair. Grinned at her.

She couldn't help grinning back.

JACE FOUGHT his way through the snow out to the barn. The snoozing horses didn't give him a second glance as he did a walk-through past each stall to ensure the animals had food and water to last until tomorrow.

The eight-week-old puppies were curled around their mama where she'd burrowed into the hay, almost blending into it. His neighbor owed him one, especially for the six trillion times Bo had asked if he could have one. Jace planned on letting his son have a dog when the boy was big enough to take care of it himself. Jace had gotten his first dog when he'd been eleven.

For a moment, his brain flashed with a memory. Amber and Bo in the barn, visiting the puppies. Amber had cuddled one in her lap as Bo had asked for a puppy for the hundredth time. When he'd said no, she'd hidden a split-second flash of disappointment by pressing her face into the dog's soft fur.

Or maybe he'd only imagined it.

Satisfied that the animals would survive the snowstorm, Jace grabbed the big box he'd hidden in the tack room, then started back through the near-blinding snow. This was a crazy storm, not the type they usually got this far south.

He was thankful for the clothesline he'd strung from the house to the barn in a "just in case" maneuver. It meant he didn't have to worry about missing the house and wandering off in the storm.

And it meant his mind could wander on the one thing it'd been stuck on all night.

Amber.

Light shone out of the living room window, illuminating a rectangle on the ground. Through the window, he could see Amber carrying an armful of gifts to the tree. She crouched down, out of sight for a moment, and then straightened, arms empty.

She stood alone in the window, one arm wrapped around her waist. Then went to the mantle, where she picked up... that funny little elf. Bo's grandma had bought it last year, and darn if he didn't forget to move that thing after Bo went to bed. Every night.

Except... Bo hadn't complained of a forgetful elf this Christmas season. He'd been full of giggles over breakfast more times than not because of the elf's silly antics. One morning he'd been incognito with Bo's action figures. Then elfie had been hiding in a cereal box in the kitchen, with just his head and shoulders visible. The elf had carried messages to Santa from Bo and had carried on a multi-day conversation in notes, always signed with a teenie flourishing signature.

All because of Amber.

Jace hadn't given it much thought, other than being thankful he didn't have to remember to move the elf every night.

And Amber hadn't mentioned it or even expected thanks. She'd brought Bo a fun Christmas experience that had resulted in joy and wonder, and she'd not expected anything for herself.

She did that a lot.

Like making some of Jace's favorite meals without being prompted. If she'd tried it once and he'd commented that he loved it, the meal appeared in the rotation.

Or doing the chores that Jace absolutely hated—laundry and vacuuming—with a joyful attitude.

Or writing the silly notes that he sometimes found in his brown-bag lunches that he took to the barn. He'd always thought she'd done them on Bo's behalf, but had she sent them just because she wanted to make him smile?

I'm interested. I have been for a while.

He'd been so blind for so long. It was a wonder she hadn't lost interest and found someone who appreciated her sooner.

Jace felt an urgency to do something for her. The gift he'd bought—suitable for a nanny, not for someone special in his life—didn't feel adequate anymore.

But it was already Christmas morning. There was no time for shopping or even making something by hand.

I don't really have family.

Her words from earlier in the evening reverberated in his brain. He'd seen the shadows pass over her face more than once tonight.

Was there something keeping Amber away from her family? If so, maybe he could help her patch things up. Wouldn't putting her family back together be an irreplaceable Christmas gift?

When snowflakes began sticking to his eyelashes and obstructing his view, he realized he'd been standing looking in the window for far too long. Amber had moved out of view. Probably waiting on him, since he'd asked.

He hurried the final few feet to the back door and bustled inside, setting down the bicycle box to stomp the snow off himself before he hung up his overcoat and took off his hat and gloves.

He reached for his toolbox, usually kept in the mudroom just below the bench, which did double-duty—a place to sit and put on boots or a catchall for this week's junk.

The toolbox wasn't there.

Please tell him it wasn't out in the barn. He remembered using it to replace a headlight on the tractor earlier in the week, but he'd thought he'd brought it back to the house.

He blew out a sigh. This night was getting longer and longer. He'd tell Amber to get some rest and put the bike together himself.

But when he carried the box into the living room, his toolbox was sitting on the coffee table, the lid open and a hammer, screwdriver and wrench all set out.

Amber.

She sat cross legged on the floor, a cup of something steaming held between her hands.

"I made you some coffee," she said with a shy smile. "Since we might be up for a while."

"Oh, I can't—"

"It's decaf. Or you can have my tea."

He stood there holding the big box, grinning like a loon. "How do you always know what I need?"

Her lashes lowered and she started to blush.

He set the box on the floor, quickly grabbing

THE NANNY'S CHRISTMAS WISH

the coffee mug to keep his hands occupied. "Are you trying to get on the naughty list? Because you promised only to distract me a little."

She glanced up at him.

He mock-glared. "You've reached your limit, young lady."

She gave him a salute, which dissolved them both into giggles.

He put down the coffee mug and reached into his pocket for his pocketknife, so he could slice open the box and get started.

He wasn't as young as he used to be. This staying up late was for the birds.

Unless he had Amber in his arms.

He almost sliced into his hand as his concentration wavered.

He pocketed the knife and pointed his index finger at her. "Young lady..." he said in a warning voice.

"What?" She was smiling. "I'm just sitting here. I'm not even doing anything."

"You just sitting here is enough."

She laughed outright. "Oh, yes. I'm very distracting in my high-class outfit." She straightened her spine and used one hand to pass over her pajamas, top to bottom. "You barely noticed me in my three-hundred-dollar dress."

She said the words as a tease. He knew it.

But was there a hint of vulnerability behind her words?

He sat on the coffee table, hands on his knees. "Amber, you're not invisible."

She sipped her tea. Hiding?

"After Patricia, I..." He shook his head. This wasn't about Patricia, not really. "I think I've been noticing you for a long time. It just took tonight to really wake me up." He held her gaze. "I don't want to go back to sleep."

CHAPTER 7

FORTY-FIVE MINUTES LATER, AMBER WATCHED AS Jace put the finishing touches on the bike. Packing Styrofoam was scattered across the floor, but they were down to the last few nuts and bolts.

By all rights, Amber should be exhausted. She never stayed up this late.

She knew Bo would be up early for Christmas.

But she was wired.

And a little afraid that if she went to bed, she'd wake up tomorrow, and this would all have been a dream.

Jace tangling his fingers with hers as she handed him the wrench.

Lifting exaggerated eyebrows as she read

each step in the directions, since he'd planned to wing it assembling the bike.

The long, hot glances he kept sending her.

It seemed surreal. Her plan had worked. Her dream was coming true. They'd agreed to take things one day at a time.

Jace *liked* her.

She covertly moved to pinch the skin between her thumb and forefinger. Ouch!

Not dreaming.

He settled the second wheel in place and held out his palm for the nut and bolt she handed him.

He was focused on his task. Casual. "You'll have to forgive me when you open my gift in the morning," he said. "I made the purchase when you were *just* the nanny." He looked up, his eyes meeting hers. "I'll make it up to you."

A thrill went through her. "Not necessary."

He went back to tightening the bolt. "As soon as I find another babysitter we can trust, we're going on a date."

She smiled. "I was going to have to protest if you hired Mrs. Ritter again. Not sure how she didn't notice him sneaking by."

"I'm just glad Bo is okay. Any ideas what

caused the reaction?"

She shrugged. "There's so much junk in those corn nuts, it could've been anything."

He winced slightly. "I get it. I'll cut down on the junk food. Maybe." He winked.

He gave the wheel a spin. Was maybe a little too casually as he said, "Something you said earlier is bugging me."

Her pulse sped. "Oh?" She'd said a lot of things tonight. Been more daring than she'd imagined she could be.

"You said you didn't have family. But you must have somebody..."

Heat flushed her face.

Jace turned the bike over in his big hands and set it on its wheels, giving it a quick roll back and forth. It moved smoothly.

And then he looked up at her. His eyes were warm, curious.

But her stomach was clenched in a tight ball.

Why had he brought this up now, when everything was going her way?

She didn't want to see the warmth in his eyes fade.

She forced a yawn. Pretended to blink sleepy

eyes at him. "Could we talk about this another time?"

Some of the openness in his gaze faded. "Is there something you don't want me to know?"

Yes.

She swallowed. Her throat felt tight and hot.

"I'd just rather talk about this sometime that's not early Christmas morning."

He sat back on his haunches. "I guess that answers my question." Suspicion and something else warred in his expression.

Her pulse pounded in her ears.

There was no *win* here. She didn't want Jace to know about her past.

She also didn't want to lose his trust.

"Jace—"

"You're right." He stood. Didn't look at her.

She followed suit.

"We should talk about this later," he finished.

But the warmth in his eyes had faded completely, and panic rose in her throat.

"There's no family," she blurted.

He went still, tension radiating from the set of his shoulders. Her panic increased.

The words were heavy in her throat. It was hard to get them out. "I grew up in foster care.

Aged out of the system. I grew up mostly in group homes."

His expression was unreadable, and her insides twisted into a knot worse than ten strands of Christmas lights.

When she'd told the other two guys she'd dated about her past, she'd seen the judgment in their eyes. Being an orphan wasn't her fault, but that didn't seem to matter.

She started to shake. "I didn't want you to know because... I was afraid you'd think I wasn't good enough to be Bo's nanny."

Mallory had been her only reference. Her previous jobs had been slinging fast food and cashiering for a big box store. She hadn't known anything about kids before she'd started working for Jace.

She waited for him to speak, heart in her throat.

He stepped toward her and closed her in his arms.

But he didn't kiss her again.

A few minutes later, after they'd said their good-nights in the hall and retired to their respective bedrooms, she lay in bed beneath the covers, shivering.

She knew every pattern in the popcorn ceiling. In the beginning, she'd lain awake at night, praying Jace wouldn't ask about her background. Afraid that he'd ask for a resume she didn't have or demand she prove her non-existent mothering skills.

She'd woken every morning before dawn to strategize how she'd spend her time with Bo, what meals she'd cook, what chores she could do around the house to distract Jace from her background.

It had seemed to work. He'd never questioned her—until now.

If she'd known that getting close to Jace would mean revealing the truth about her past, would she have stayed home? Saved her money and not bought the red dress?

She didn't know anything anymore.

Only how empty she felt.

Now that he knew her lack of qualifications, would he demand she leave the ranch?

She couldn't bear the thought of saying goodbye to Bo—or to Jace.

Maybe if she begged, he'd allow her to stay on.

But she was deeply afraid that he would never

again look at her with the warmth he'd shown tonight.

Jace had made a mistake.

He'd known it when he'd held a trembling Amber in his arms. After what she'd revealed, he hadn't known what to say to fix it. So he'd said nothing.

He knew better.

Now he forced himself up and out of his warm bed. He couldn't get to sleep anyway.

He threw on a pair of jeans and a second thermal shirt. He crept through the quiet house and paused in the mudroom to don his heavy coat and boots.

The snow hadn't let up any, and he used the line to the barn again as he crossed the yard.

He went to the pen where he'd put the dog and her puppies. Stood there staring down at the sleeping animals.

Seriously, he should be in the poem. Everyone was sleeping, and he was the mouse.

He'd been kidding himself before when he'd convinced himself he imagined Amber's reaction to the puppies.

She'd wanted one but had hidden her disappointment for Jace's sake.

And now it made sense. If she'd grown up in group homes, she'd never have owned a pet.

He still remembered being fourteen and finally talking his parents into sending him to the Triple T ranch for the first time. He'd found himself on the back of a horse. Known a camaraderie with the animal that had been special.

Amber had never had that. Had never had any kind of real security.

And tonight, he'd botched things. Probably made her feel worse.

Part of him wanted to go and wake her up, beg her forgiveness for being stupid.

The sane part of him said it'd have to wait until the morning.

She had to know what she meant to Bo. Jace's son would be devastated if she ever left.

And he'd thought he'd made his feelings plain during their time tonight.

But was that enough for someone like Amber? Someone who'd been moved around at the whims of a bureaucratic system? He hadn't told her he was falling for her. He'd told her they should take it a day at a time.

He'd be lucky if she'd give him the time of day come tomorrow morning.

Unless... could he give her a perfect Christmas morning? Deliver a present that would show her exactly where she belonged— here, with him and Bo?

He stared at the puppies a little longer, contemplating how he could pull this off.

He'd never made a big gesture with Patricia. She'd known him too well, and they'd been together since high school. He'd never *had* to. Maybe if they'd had more time, maybe he'd have eventually dug himself a hole so deep it would've taken a monumental gesture to get back in her good graces.

Patricia was gone. Amber was here.

And it was time to man-up. Admit to the feelings he had for her.

If that meant giving her a Christmas she'd never forget, then that's what he would do.

CHAPTER 8

AMBER WAS AVOIDING HIM.

At least that what it felt like early the next morning. She hadn't come out of her room, even though Bo was making a holy ruckus about the bike.

"I can't believe Santa got here in that wicked snowstorm." Bo sat on the bike, struggling to pedal on the living room carpet.

"Rudolph must've had his nose turned on high-beam," Jace returned. "How about I make some coffee before we open presents? Give Amber some time to wake up?"

Because he wanted her to do this with them. Needed her to be there.

He put the coffeepot on, then stood at the counter, staring at the winter wonderland outside the window. Yesterday's storm had brought almost a foot of pristine white powder.

Except where his footprints from this morning's errand to the barn had disrupted the white blanket. He'd thought of the perfect gift after all. It was now hidden in his bedroom, waiting for the right moment.

He just needed Amber to accept it.

He was no longer afraid of what might happen if a relationship with Amber went badly.

He was already in deep enough that if she decided to leave him, there would be a fair amount of grief involved.

So he'd determined to do everything he could to make her want to stay.

For good.

The scent of coffee wafted through the room. The machine stopped brewing, and the last of the coffee dripped into the pot.

Bo wouldn't wait for long.

"C'mon, Dad!" came the call from the living room.

Speaking of.

Choosing to be optimistic, Jace poured two mugs of coffee and carried them with him.

When he hit the living room, Bo was pulling

Amber by the hand from the hallway.

"She was awake!" Bo crowed. "I knocked and everything, just to be polite."

At least his son hadn't cannonballed onto her bed the way he'd woken Jace this morning. He sent her a chagrined smile.

Her return smile was too quick. He barely caught it before it faded. Like last night, her gaze bounced away from his.

No way.

He wasn't letting his Christmas miracle escape.

He strode directly toward her, detouring only to set the mugs on the coffee table. Though she'd stopped behind the couch, Bo still held her hand, as if he—like Jace—thought she was going to make a run for it.

"Why don't you see what's in your stocking?" he told his son.

"Yes!" Bo abandoned his hold on Amber and raced around the couch, toward the floor in front of the tree where his Christmas sock bulged with goodies. He didn't look back.

Amber watched the boy with a small smile playing around her mouth. But when her gaze met Jace's, it was full of uncertainty.

That had to go.

He didn't care that Bo was in the room. This couldn't wait.

He closed the distance between them and swept her into his arms, brushing kisses on her cheek and forehead before seeking her lips. He kissed her until they were both breathless and she was clinging to his shoulders.

Then he leaned his forehead against hers.

Somewhere behind him, Bo was exclaiming over the small gifts from his stocking.

When Jace's eyes finally came into focus, he saw a single tear falling down her cheek.

He cupped her face, let his thumb sweep it away.

"Christmas morning is a time for families," he whispered. "You're a part of ours."

He saw the hope spring to her eyes. Saw her quickly bank it.

"You were right last night. It was late. If I'd had any brain cells left, I would've said something about how incredible you've been with Bo for the last eighteen months. It doesn't seem to matter that you didn't have a mother, because you're a natural." He shrugged. "Maybe spending so much time with other kids taught you how to

be a good mom. It's the little things, you know."
He lowered his voice. "Like elves. Bo sees you as
more than his nanny. And I do, too."

Another tear rolled down her cheek, and this
time, he kissed it away.

And heard, "Whoa! Are you guys kissing?"

He turned, keeping Amber in his arms, to find
Bo jumping on the couch.

Before he could even ask what his son
thought, Bo was flinging both arms above
his head.

"Yes! This is the best Christmas ever!"

Amber giggled and Jace squeezed her waist.
He brushed a kiss into her hair.

"I guess that answers that."

AMBER STOOD in the circle of Jace's arms, her lips
still tingling from his kisses. She couldn't stop
smiling, even if her heart was pounding out of
her chest.

Bo went flying off the couch with a
war whoop.

She turned her face up to Jace's. "If you want
to know more about my childhood, I'll tell you."

He deserved know everything about the

woman who was taking care of his son.

Maybe she'd been wrong to keep her past a secret all this time. She'd thought she was protecting herself, but...

Sometime during the sleepless night, she'd decided that her past didn't define her. She'd come through it, bruised and scarred in some ways, but she could choose how to act, who to be *now*.

Jace nuzzled the place where her neck met her shoulder, sending a delicious shiver down her spine.

"I want to know everything about you," he said, his lips burning her bare skin. "When you're ready to tell me."

That was sweet.

And so was his kiss.

Last night, she'd thought she'd lost the chance to be with Jace like this. She'd never been so glad to be wrong in her entire life.

"Enough kissing!" Bo's voice broke through the perfect moment.

Maybe made it perfect in another way.

Jace smiled against her mouth, and then she was smiling, too.

"Da-ad! Amber! Presents!"

And then Bo was there, burrowing into the little space between them. For a moment, he seemed content to be part of a three-way hug, but it didn't last.

He bounded away, climbed over the back of the couch. "Please!"

With a laugh, Jace finally let her go.

That was all right.

Because she saw the look he sent her way. There would be more kisses later.

Good-night kisses.

Good-morning kisses.

Secret kisses, snuck as she ducked into the laundry room.

Maybe one day... wedding kisses?

Jace grinned as if he were reading her mind. "All right, all right. But since Santa's already delivered you a big one, I think we should let Amber open the first gift."

She crossed the room, aiming for the mug of coffee Jace had brought. "That's not—"

"Sit." Jace pointed an index finger at her.

Bo was bouncing on his toes, his eyes wide and excited.

She folded her legs beneath her and took a

spot between the coffee table and the Christmas tree.

But instead of going to the tree and the massive pile of gifts beneath, Jace disappeared down the hall, Bo trailing him.

Strange.

She sipped her coffee, getting a little lost in a daydream of the New Year's Eve kisses she might receive.

Until a tiny *jingle, jingle, jingle* brought her back to the present.

A golden-haired puppy raced from the hallway in a zigzag pattern.

She barely had time to stash her coffee on the table before it careened into her lap, stumbling on paws that were one size too big.

She picked it up, tubby tummy and all. "Who're you?"

The puppy immediately started licking her chin.

The single bell that had been attached to a red ribbon around his neck jangled as she nuzzled her nose against the puppy's.

"Jace, what—?"

Man and boy stood just beyond the hallway,

watching with matching broad smiles. Jace had one hand resting on his son's shoulder.

"A family doesn't seem like a family without a dog," Jace said.

He nudged Bo toward the Christmas tree and sat next to her, letting his long legs stretch out on the floor. He took something out of his pocket.

He looked a little... nervous.

The puppy tumbled out of her lap and onto the floor between them.

"Here," Jace extended a small red collar to her. "Put it on him."

Now he sounded nervous.

She laughed as the puppy tried to wrestle her hands as she untied the jingle bell ribbon.

Jace clasped her hand when she reached for the collar. She looked up to fall into his eyes.

"This collar is a token of my promise to you."

She started to smile. He sounded so serious. Like he was saying *vows*—

Her breath caught in her chest as the enormity of what was happening hit.

Jace squeezed her hand in his.

"With this collar, I promise that he—and you, will always have a home here. Not only in my house, but in my heart."

She couldn't help the single tear that dripped down her cheek..

He was offering her so much more than she'd dared to hope for.

A home. His heart.

A family.

"I accept," she whispered. She leaned in, and Jace met her with a sweet kiss.

"Aaah, enough kissing!" But Bo was laughing.

And then a tiny growl preceded the puppy grabbing the hem of her shirt in his razor teeth and playing tug of war.

She broke away from Jace, laughing.

He chuckled, too, as he disengaged the puppy from her pajamas and quickly secured the collar on the squirming, wiggly body.

"All right, Bo. Presents. Go ahead."

The boy dove for the tree with abandon. The puppy quickly followed suit, sniffing the artificial branches.

Jace scooted until they were shoulder-to-shoulder.

Amber had never felt such deep contentment as this.

She watched as Bo ripped open wrapping paper from his gifts. The puppy wrestled and fought with the discarded paper and ribbons, clumsy with his big puppy feet.

And Jace wrapped his arm around her shoulders as they sipped their coffees.

She'd force herself away to give him his gift soon.

Maybe.

She felt like she could stay here forever.

He tipped his head toward hers. "He's going to need a name."

She considered the pup. "What about Prancer? After the reindeer."

She saw Jace's nose wrinkle out of the corner of her eye.

"If you want him to get beat up by all the other dogs. What about Buck? Or Kujo?"

She laughed. "There's no way something this fluffy is a Kujo."

"Grinch?" Jace suggested next.

"He's got too much Christmas spirit to be the Grinch."

Bo had set a used self-adhesive bow on top of the dog's head, and it shook and growled until the puppy pitched forward and rolled.

Bo dissolved into little-boy giggles.

Jace's thumb traced a pattern on her shoulder.

"I'm definitely feeling like the Grinch on Christmas morning," he confessed. "My heart's too big for my chest."

She turned to gaze up into his face. "Me too."

"Want to know the only thing that could make this moment better?" He leaned toward her.

She nodded, expecting him to close the distance and kiss her.

But the sparkle in his eye said different. "My Christmas gift."

She laughed even as the puppy attacked her sock, catching her toe with his sharp teeth.

Jace joined in the fun, starting a tickle war that Bo was quick to join in.

They only stopped when she was pinned beneath Jace on the floor in the middle of wrapping paper mess.

Well, Bo was lying across his dad, still pounding his fists.

Jace's hands pinned her wrists to the floor.

Jace looked down on her with dancing eyes. "Do you surrender?"

Her heart? It'd been his for a long time.

The tickle war was another matter. In her

peripheral vision, she saw the puppy gearing up for a pounce—on Jace's ear.

As he moved to protect his head from puppy teeth and claws, Amber freed her arms to tickle his sides.

He arched away, then returned with a roar. Bo laughed, arms coming around his dad's shoulders.

And Amber soon found herself in Jace's lap, barred in by his arms. The puppy had been distracted by a ribbon and bow.

Jace blew hot air on her ear, and she shivered.

"Surrender," he said.

She turned her head, her hair catching in his morning scruff.

"I'm already yours."

His lips were in her direct line of sight. She watched his smile spread. This dear man.

She was well and caught. And she never wanted to get loose again.

ALSO BY LACY WILLIAMS

SNOWBOUND IN SAWYER CREEK SERIES
(CONTEMPORARY ROMANCE)

Soldier Under the Mistletoe

The Nanny's Christmas Wish

The Rancher's Unexpected Gift

WILD WYOMING HEART SERIES
(HISTORICAL ROMANCE)

Marrying Miss Marshal

Counterfeit Cowboy

Cowboy Pride

Courted by a Cowboy

TRIPLE H BRIDES SERIES (CONTEMPORARY
ROMANCE)

Kissing Kelsey

Courting Carrie

Stealing Sarah

Keeping Kayla

Melting Megan

COWBOY FAIRYTALES SERIES
(CONTEMPORARY ROMANCE)

Once Upon a Cowboy

Cowboy Charming

The Toad Prince

The Beastly Princess

The Lost Princess

HEART OF OKLAHOMA SERIES
(CONTEMPORARY ROMANCE)

Kissed by a Cowboy

Love Letters from Cowboy

Mistletoe Cowboy

Cowgirl for Keeps

Jingle Bell Cowgirl

Heart of a Cowgirl

3 Days with a Cowboy

Prodigal Cowgirl

Made in the USA
Coppell, TX
29 May 2021